For Joseph, Daniel, Adam, and David,
for the days when you fell asleep
in my arms —JB

For Rowan and Griffin, Delilah and
Watson, and Faye —JZ

ABOUT THIS BOOK
The illustrations for this book were done in graphite
on vellum bristol paper and colored digitally. This book
was edited by Deirdre Jones, art directed by David Caplan,
and designed by Prashansa Thapa. The production was supervised by
Nyamekye Waliyaya, and the production editor was Marisa Finkelstein.
The text was set in ITC Quorum, and the display type is hand lettered.

Library of Congress Cataloging-in-Publication Data • Names: Berry, Julie, 1974– author. | Zollars, Jaime, illustrator. • Title: The night frolic / written by Julie Berry ; illustrated by Jaime Zollars. • Description: First edition. | New York, NY : Little, Brown and Company, 2023. | Audience: Ages 4–8. | Summary: "Before they go to sleep, children travel on a dreamy, whimsical journey to visit the Night Tiger, the Night Walrus, the Night Elephant, and others." —Provided by publisher. • Identifiers: LCCN 2020048665 | ISBN 9780316591836 (hardcover) • Subjects: CYAC: Bedtime—Fiction. | Night—Fiction. | Dreams—Fiction. • Classification: LCC PZ7.B461747 Nig 2022 | DDC [E]—dc23 • LC record available at https://lccn.loc.gov/2020048665 • ISBN 978-0-316-59183-6 • PRINTED IN CHINA • APS • 10 9 8 7 6 5 4 3 2 1

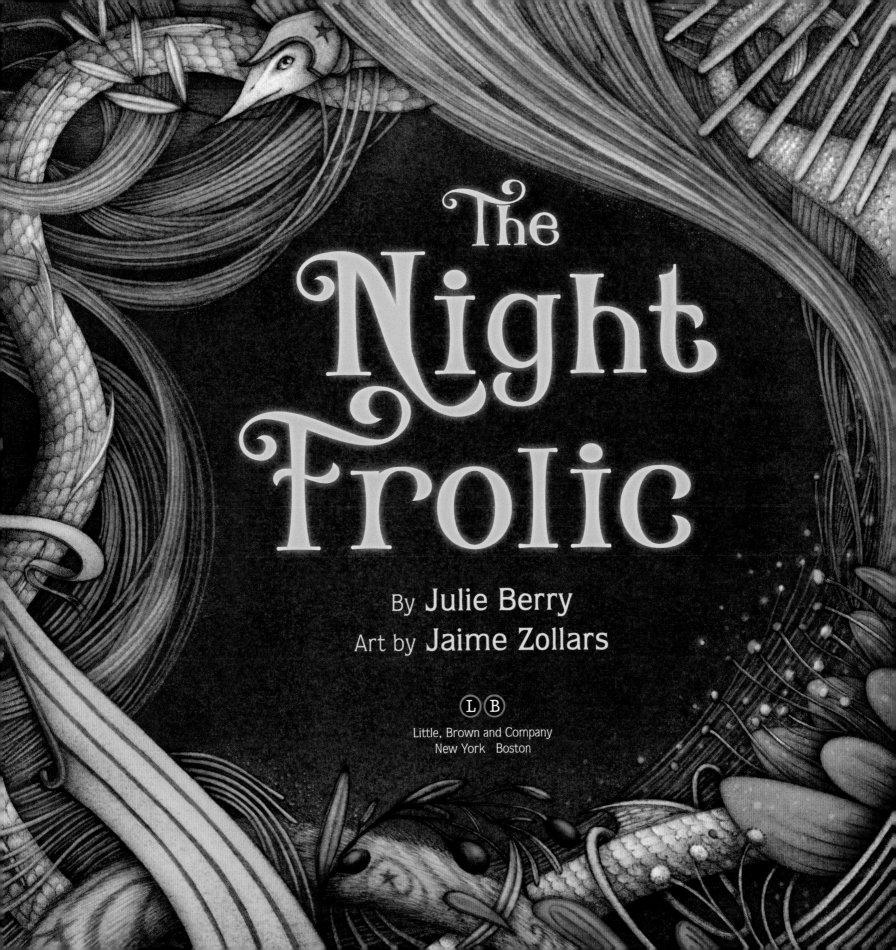

The Night Frolic

By **Julie Berry**

Art by **Jaime Zollars**

L B

Little, Brown and Company
New York   Boston

Where do children go when they drift off to sleep?

They float on a warm nighttime breeze over forests and peaks to the high den of the Night Tiger.

"Good evening, children," she purrs.
"Are you ready?"

The children and the Tiger's cubs tumble down
a mountain carpeted in night blossoms
and arrive at the moonlit sea.

"Greetings, children," says the Moon.
"Are you coming?"

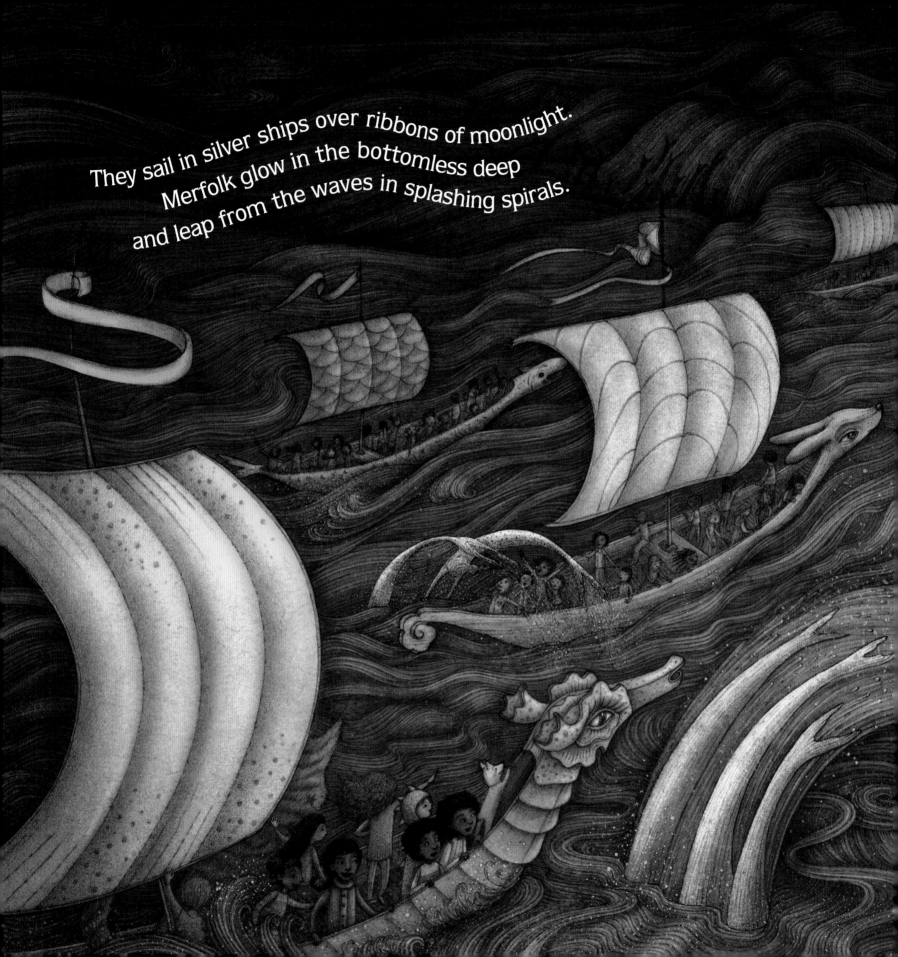

They sail in silver ships over ribbons of moonlight.
Merfolk glow in the bottomless deep
and leap from the waves in splashing spirals.

"Welcome, children,"
they sing.

"Are you joyful?"

The ships weave through mighty icebergs shimmering in the starlight. Bears romp, and seals splash . . .

. . . then they all bow to the Night Walrus.
"A good night to you, children," he barks.
"Do you feel the music?"

The ships reach the beach at the top of the world,
where colored lights dance in the sky.

The earth's great pole holds up a shining pavilion.
At its entry stands the Night Elephant.

"The children are here!" she trumpets.
"At last, the Night Frolic can begin!"

The children grab
drums and cymbals,
horns and flutes,
guitars and fiddles,
batons and sparklers.

Round the great tent
they march and twirl.
All the beasts and
lovely creatures join in.

The Night Elephant
    throws back the curtains,
        and the Night Frolic spills out.

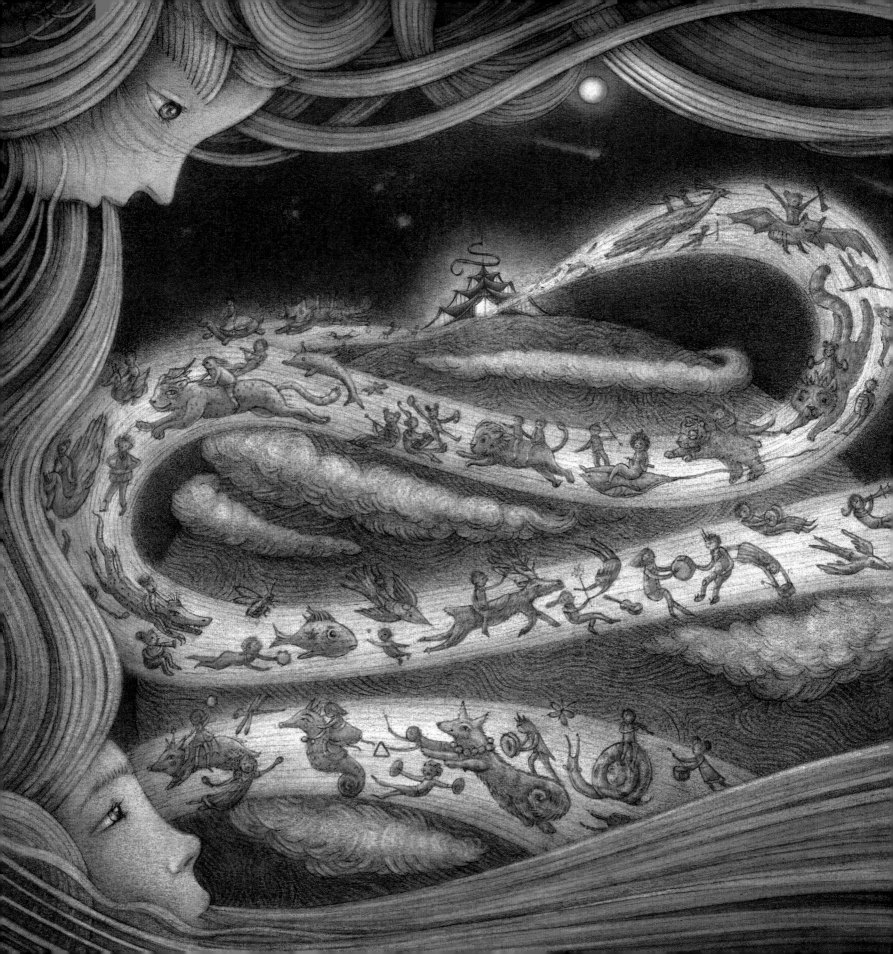

Sailing, soaring,
somersaulting,
the children skim
over sea and sand
until their Night Frolic
stirs the stars in the sky.
The Four Winds spread
the children's song.

The music awakens the Old Serpent
that encircles the world.

He smiles down upon them.
"Blessssssings on you, children," he whispers.
"Issssssn't it time for you to ssssssssleep?"

Down toward the dark sea the children glide, where they ride upon dolphins to their home shores.

The warm nighttime breeze
lifts the children
and tucks them into their soft beds.

The Night Tiger gathers
her cubs close in her den.

The Moon sinks into the sea.
The merfolk rest in ocean caves.

The Night Walrus tells the seals a bedtime story.

The Night Elephant nibbles on a peanut.
The swirling stars dance on and on.

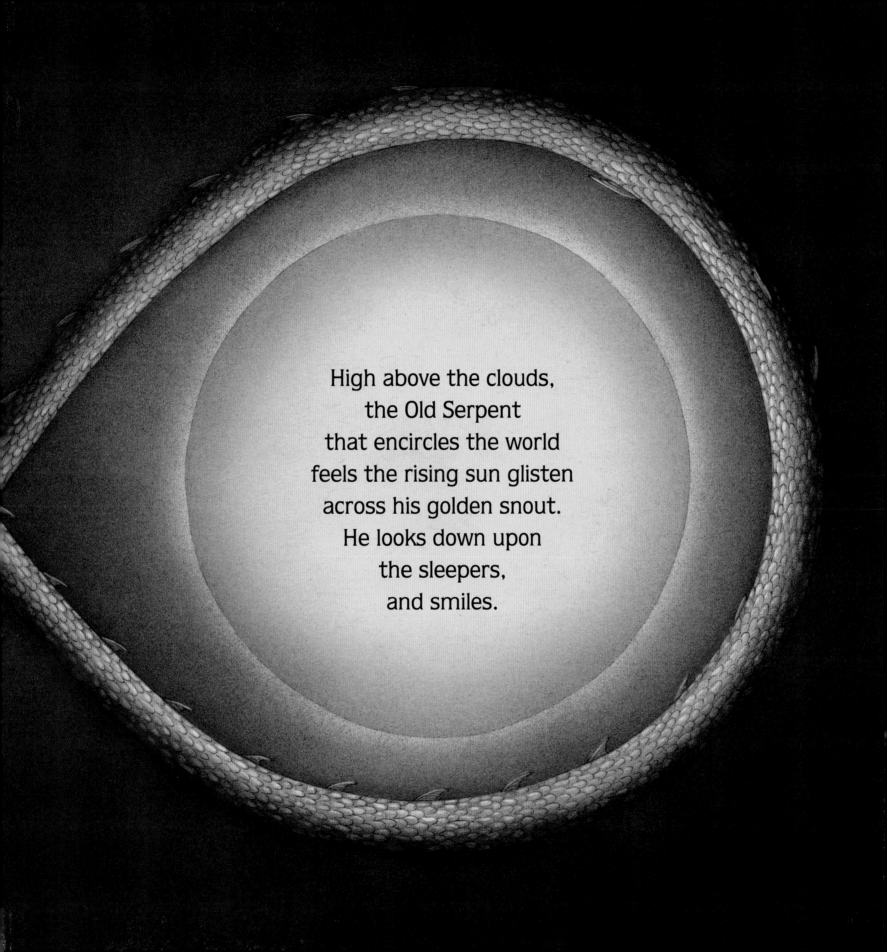

High above the clouds,
the Old Serpent
that encircles the world
feels the rising sun glisten
across his golden snout.
He looks down upon
the sleepers,
and smiles.

"Good morning, children," he whispers.
"Are you ready?"